D0513729

First American Edition.

Published in the United States by Grolier Enterprises Inc., Danbury, Connecticut.
Originally published in Denmark as JAFAR VENDER TILBAGE
by Egmont Gruppen, Copenhagen.

ISBN: 0-7172-8495-6
Manufactured in the United States of America.

B C D 6 7 8 9

Disney's

The Return of Jafar

GROLIER
BOOK CLUB EDITION

Once upon an Arabian night a band of thieves stole a wonderful treasure.

"Not bad for one night's work!" said their leader. His name was Abis Mal.

he thieves didn’t know they were being watched!

Suddenly a furry hand shot out of the darkness. It belonged to a monkey named Abu.

Abu plucked a flower-shaped jewel from the treasure.

"Thief! Put that back!" shouted one of the robbers.

Just then Aladdin swept down on his Magic Carpet.

He scooped up Abu and all the treasure, too.

Then away they flew to the city of Agrabah!

Aladdin gave the treasure to the poor people.
But he saved the flower-shaped jewel for
Princess Jasmine.

Meanwhile, far out in the desert, a parrot burst out of a magic lamp! The parrot's name was Iago.

"Iago, get me out of this lamp!" shouted a voice. It belonged to Iago's cruel master, Jafar.

Iago did not want to free Jafar—ever! So he dropped the lamp down a well and flew away.

Once, after being tricked by Iago and Jafar, Aladdin had found a different lamp. The kindhearted Genie who lived inside it helped Aladdin win Princess Jasmine's heart.

Jafar had tried to steal the throne from Princess Jasmine's father, the Sultan. But Aladdin had come to the Sultan's rescue.

Then Jafar got hold of Aladdin's lamp. He wished to be a powerful genie.

Jafar got his wish.

But he forgot where genies have to live. He and Iago were pulled down into a lamp!

The Genie had thrown the lamp far into the desert.

Now Jafar was at the bottom of a well. But Iago was back in Agrabah.

Aladdin and Abu were crossing the square when they saw the parrot.

"Iago, what are *you* doing here?" Aladdin asked.

Just then Abis Mal spotted Aladdin.
"There's the boy who stole our gold!" he shouted to his men.
The thieves attacked!

“If I don’t do something, I could get hurt,” Iago said. So he dropped a potted plant on a board and sent Abis Mal flying.

The thieves ran away, and Aladdin was saved.

Aladdin was grateful.

"Iago," he said, "I've misjudged you. You're not such a bad fellow after all!"

Iago smiled. No one had ever said such a nice thing to him before. Certainly not his former master, Jafar!

That afternoon Aladdin gave Princess Jasmine the jewel. Suddenly they heard a familiar voice.

"I'm back!" the voice called. It was their friend, the Genie!

He showed them all the wonderful places he'd seen.

Aladdin and Jasmine wanted to travel around the world, too!

At that moment all Abis Mal wanted was water. He went to a well and pulled up the bucket.

"What's this lamp doing in here?" he asked.

Abis Mal rubbed the lamp to dry it. Out came a towering genie!

"I am free at last!" thundered Jafar.

Jafar changed back into his human form. He didn't want to frighten Abis Mal.

"You are now my master," Jafar told the thief. "You may have three wishes."

Abis Mal quickly wished for the treasure of a legendary sunken ship.

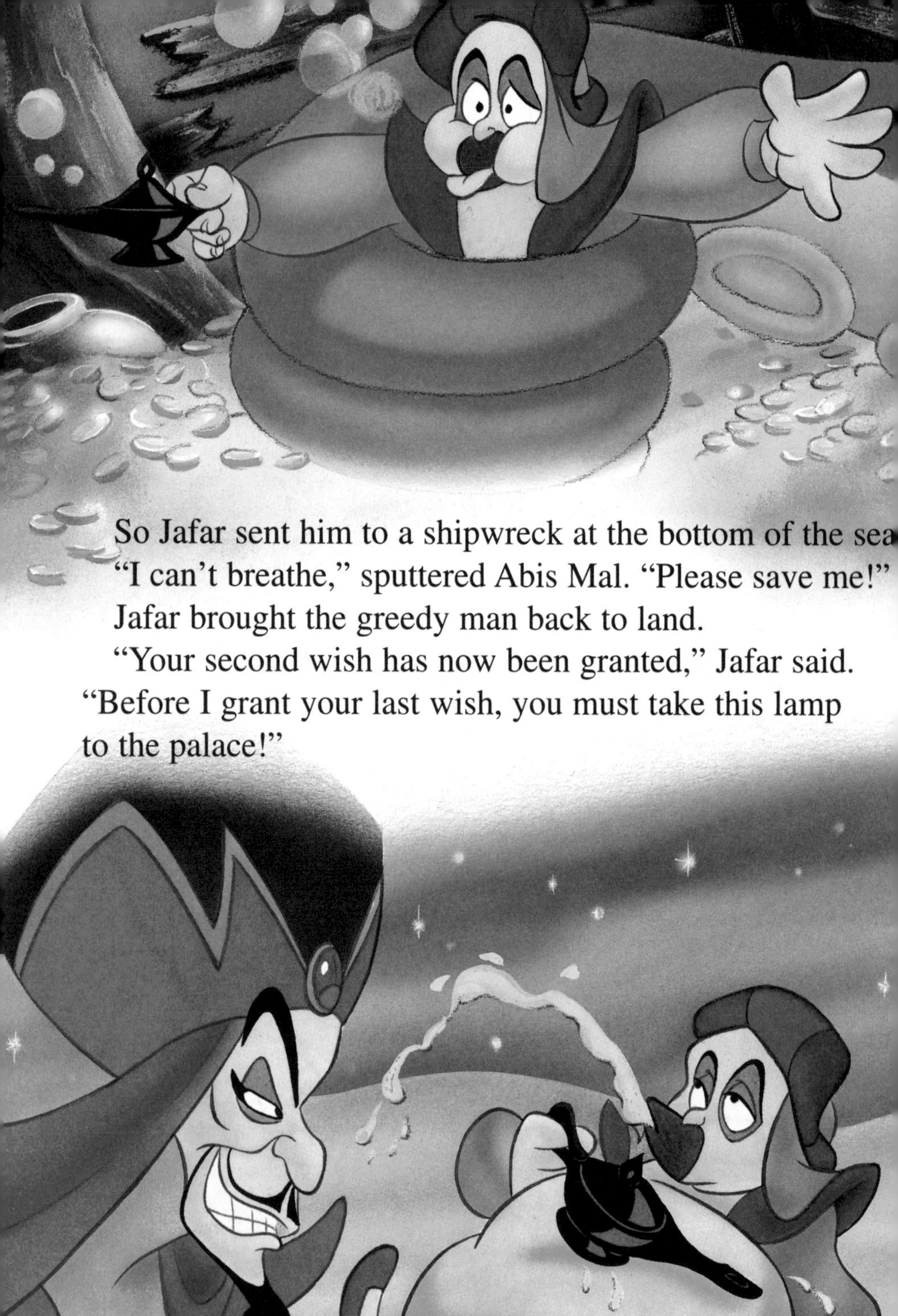

So Jafar sent him to a shipwreck at the bottom of the sea.
"I can't breathe," sputtered Abis Mal. "Please save me!"
Jafar brought the greedy man back to land.
"Your second wish has now been granted," Jafar said. "Before I grant your last wish, you must take this lamp to the palace!"

Aladdin was at the palace with the Sultan.

"Please forgive Iago," said Aladdin. "He saved my life."

"I will pardon Iago," replied the Sultan. "But you will be in charge of him. If that parrot gets into any more trouble, I will blame you."

That evening Abis Mal crept into the palace. He put the magic lamp on a table beside Iago.

Jafar flew out of the lamp in a huge cloud of smoke. "Your master is back," he said to the startled parrot. "If you wish to live, you will do as I say. You must get the Sultan and Aladdin out of the palace."

Iago was afraid of Jafar. So the next day he spoke with Aladdin. “Perhaps the Sultan would like to take a ride on your Magic Carpet,” he said.

“What a splendid idea,” Aladdin replied.

Soon he and the Sultan were flying high above the desert.

"Good!" cried Jafar. "The Sultan and Aladdin are gone. It is time to deal with Aladdin's friends!"

Jafar took the Genie by surprise.

The Genie fought back. But after a brave struggle he was defeated.

Jafar trapped the Genie inside a glass ball. Then he locked Abu in chains.

Iago felt terrible. His new friends were in danger—and it was all his fault!

Jafar sent for Abis Mal. "These flying horses are for you and your men. Use them to capture the Sultan," he ordered.

Aladdin did his best to protect the Sultan, but it was no use.

Abis Mal's men seized the Sultan.

Then Jafar turned a river into a rising funnel. Aladdin was pulled down, down into the raging water!

Next the evil Jafar captured Jasmine.
"Thanks for your help," he said to Iago.
"Soon I will have total revenge on Aladdin."

Jasmine and her father glared
at the guilty parrot.

Iago had never felt
so ashamed!

At last, Aladdin finally
made it back to the palace.

But the palace guards were waiting for him! "You have kidnapped the Sultan!" they shouted. "Now you will pay with your life!"

The palace guards arrested Aladdin.
Jafar's plan was working perfectly!

Iago felt so guilty! This was all his fault. But what could a parrot do?

Suddenly he had an idea.

Iago picked up the glass ball with the Genie inside. Then he dropped it on the floor!

The ball shattered, and out flew the Genie.

"I'm off to save Aladdin!" he cried.

He got there in the nick of time!

Jafar was furious! He became a genie again. "How many times do I have to get rid of you!" Jafar shouted at the Genie.

He attacked the Genie with all his might. Again, the Genie was no match for the evil Jafar.

"The lamp!" cried Aladdin. "To get rid of Jafar, I must destroy it!"

Next Jafar became a wild volcano. Everything he touched turned to fiery liquid.

Then Jafar saw Aladdin reach for the lamp. So he melted the ground all around him.

Aladdin couldn't reach the lamp!

Iago decided he had to help his new friends.

The brave little bird snatched the lamp and then dropped it.

Down, down, down it tumbled, into the bubbling lava.

The lamp melted before their eyes.
Then it was gone.
And in that instant Jafar was gone, too!

Everyone returned to the palace.

The grateful Sultan made Aladdin his special adviser. And he took very good care of Iago.

Now that the kingdom was safe, Aladdin and Jasmine flew off on the Magic Carpet.

It was time for them to see the world!